BOBBY CLARKE

JEREMY ROENICK

RON HEXTALL

BOB KELLY

BERNIE PARENT

REGGIE LEACH

JOHN LeCLAIR

RICK TOCCHET

TIM KERR

ERIC LINDROS

RICK MacLEISH

MARK RECCHI

The History of the

PHILADELPHIA FLYERS

John Nichols

CREATIVE EDUCATION

Published by Creative Education, 123 South Broad Street, Mankato, MN 56001

Creative Education is an imprint of The Creative Company.

Designed by Rita Marshall.

Photographs by Getty Images (Victor Decolognon/NHLI, Dave Sandford/NHLI),

Hockey Hall of Fame (Paul Bereswill, Graphic Artists, London Life-Portnoy),

Sports Gallery Inc. (Al Messerschmidt), SportsChrome USA (Gregg Forwerck)

Library of Congress Cataloging-in-Publication Data

Nichols, John, 1966– The history of the Philadelphia Flyers / by John Nichols.

p. cm. — (Stanley Cup champions) ISBN 1-58341-279-4

Summary: A history of Philadelphia's winning hockey team from its

first season in 1967 to the present.

1. Philadelphia Flyers (Hockey team)—Juvenile literature.

[1. Philadelphia Flyers (Hockey team)—History.] I. Title. II. Series.

GV848.P48 N53 2003 796.962'64'0974811—dc21 2002034761

First Edition 9 8 7 6 5 4 3 2 1

PHILADELPHIA, PENNSYLVANIA, IS ONE OF THE MOST HISTORICALLY RICH CITIES IN THE UNITED STATES. PHILADELPHIA DATES BACK TO THE TIME OF THE American Revolution and the Declaration of Independence, when citizens of the "City of Brotherly Love" fiercely fought for freedom against the British. Times have changed, but Philadelphians are still famous for their fierce devotion to the city's many historical sites and renowned universities.

Philadelphians are also fanatical about their sports teams. Long known for loyally backing less than stellar teams in professional baseball, football, and basketball, Philadelphia fans finally got a winner when the National Hockey League (NHL) awarded the city an expansion team in 1967. Named the Flyers, the Philadelphia club was soon soaring among the league's elite.

ANDRE LaCROIX

{SUDDEN SUCCESS WITH CLARKE} Philadelphia was one of six teams that joined the NHL before the 1967–68 season. Like most expansion teams, the first Flyers roster was a collection of inexperienced and aging players. However, unlike most expansion teams, the first-year Flyers, led by center Andre LaCroix and wings Gary Dornhoefer and Leon Rochefort, played solid team hockey and posted a 31–32–11 record to capture the West Division title and make the playoffs.

The Flyers suffered their worst loss ever in January **1969**, losing 12–0 to the Chicago Blackhawks.

The Flyers were knocked out in the first round of the playoffs by the St. Louis Blues, but the team's hustling style of play and never-say-die attitude struck a chord with Philadelphia fans. That style and attitude would carry the team far, as the feisty Flyers would make the postseason in 22 of their first 23 seasons.

A huge part of the Flyers' early success was the outstanding

KEITH PRIMEAU

PRIME
25
cing
RELESS

BOBBY CLARKE

Feisty and fearless Flyers great Bobby Clarke played in nine NHL All-Star Games.

play of center Bobby Clarke. When he joined the team in 1969 at the age of 20, many people thought he was too small (5-foot-10 and 180 pounds) and wouldn't be able to overcome the effects of diabetes—a disease that affects the body's blood sugar levels. The fiery Clarke quickly proved his critics wrong. In the 1970–71 season, he scrapped and hustled his way to 63 points (goals plus assists). Two seasons later, Clarke was one of the elite players in the league, piling up 104 points.

In **1972–73**, Rick MacLeish became the eighth player in NHL history to score 50 goals in a season.

The Flyers began to develop several other outstanding players as well. Wingers Rick MacLeish and Bill Barber, along with defenseman Joe Watson, helped the Flyers build momentum in the early '70s. Philadelphia's victory totals rose dramatically, going from 17 in Clarke's rookie year to 37 in 1972–73.

Clearly, the Flyers were on the verge of great things. "We've

RICK MacLEISH

Like Bobby Clarke, defenseman Eric Desjardins led the Flyers as team captain.

ERIC DESJARDINS

got a lot of the pieces here to win a championship," said Clarke after the Flyers were eliminated by the Montreal Canadiens in the 1973 playoffs. "We just have to find the edge that will take us to the top."

Starting with the **1972–73** season, the Flyers treated their fans to 16 winning seasons in a row.

{THE BROAD STREET BULLIES} Another key factor in the Flyers' quick rise to contention was head coach Fred Shero. Hired in 1970, Shero seemed an odd fit as a hockey coach. Quiet, and with the looks of a college professor, Shero was known to quote classic literature and write odd inspirational phrases on the locker room blackboards. Because of his strange ways, Shero was nicknamed "Freddie the Fog." Although the Fog's actions were sometimes odd, his coaching philosophy was as simple as a punch in the nose. "Take the shortest route to the puck, and arrive in ill humor," was one of the coach's favorite sayings.

The style of play in the NHL during the 1970s was very

BOB KELLY

physical, with fights a common occurrence. Every team was tough, but Shero's Flyers were the toughest. Players such as center Orest Kindrachuk and wings Dave "the Hammer" Schultz and Bob

"Hound" Kelly helped the Flyers earn the nickname "The Broad Street Bullies" (Broad being the street that ran in front of the Spectrum, Philadelphia's home arena).

In 1973–74, the Flyers muscled their way to a 50–16–12 record. In the playoffs, the team rode the hot goaltending of Bernie Parent all the way to the Stanley Cup Finals, where it met the mighty Boston Bruins. The series was a physical struggle, with both teams taking their lumps. Going into the sixth game, Philadelphia was one win away from the championship. Playing on home ice, Parent and the Flyers stonewalled Boston 1–0 to become the first of the six expansion teams to claim the Stanley Cup.

> Bernie Parent won the Conn Smythe Trophy (as the playoffs' top player) in **1974** and **1975**.

The Flyers added more scoring punch the next season by acquiring wing Reggie Leach. Known for his thunderous slap shot, Leach notched 45 goals playing with Clarke and Barber on the team's top line. With yet another weapon in their arsenal, the Flyers rolled to another Stanley Cup in 1975, this time beating the Buffalo Sabres in the finals. "It's tough to win one championship," said

BERNIE PARENT

SHER-WOOD
SHER-WOOD

Clarke. "But to go back-to-back puts us in the history books."

{THE BULLIES BOW OUT} In 1975–76, Leach scored 60 goals, and Clarke captured the last of his three Hart Trophies as the

league's Most Valuable Player. But the Flyers' championship reign ended when the Montreal Canadiens tamed the Broad Street Bullies in a four-game Stanley Cup Finals sweep.

As the '70s wore on, the Flyers kept the core of their championship teams intact. Clarke, Leach, and Rick MacLeish were still effective, and new additions such as bruising wing Paul Holmgren and center Mel Bridgeman helped the Flyers remain a contender. Unfortunately for Philadelphia fans, the Flyers of the late 1970s and early '80s were overshadowed by two of the greatest dynasties in NHL history—the Montreal Canadiens (four straight Stanley Cups from 1976 to 1979) and the New York Islanders (four straight Cups from 1980 to 1983).

With his stellar work in the nets, goalie Roman Cechmanek reminded fans of Bernie Parent.

In 1980, the Flyers had their best chance to unseat one of the big powers. Facing the Islanders in the Stanley Cup Finals, the Flyers won games two and five but lost the series in game six when New York won in overtime, 5–4. "Looking back, that was the last hurrah for Bobby, Reggie, and all those guys from the Bullies," said Flyers

R. CECHMANEK

00-GO-
VANBIESBROUCK
34
CCM
BROWN
SHER-WOOD

Mikael Renberg was one of many hard-hitting wings to wear the black and orange.

center Ken Linseman. "I was 22, and I thought it was the beginning of something. Really, it was the beginning of the end."

Tim Kerr set a Flyers franchise record with 17 hat tricks (games with three or more goals).

By the end of the 1983–84 season, it was all over for Clarke, Leach, MacLeish, and the rest of the championship Flyers. Clarke left the game as the Flyers' all-time leading scorer with 352 goals and 852 assists. The heart and soul of the organization nearly since its start, Clarke went on to become the team's general manager and president.

{BEASTS OF THE EAST} With the era of the Broad Street Bullies over, a new cast of Flyers heroes began to emerge in the mid-1980s. Heady defenseman Mark Howe and talented goalie Pelle Lindbergh anchored the defense, while wingers Rick Tocchet and Brian Propp provided much of the offense. These Flyers played the same bone-rattling, hardworking style that Philly fans loved. One

TIM KERR

player in particular brought back memories of the Flyers' rough-and-tumble roots: hulking wing Tim Kerr.

Kerr was a 6-foot-3 and 225-pound mountain of a man known

to anchor himself in front of the opposing team's goal and use his strength and quick hands to collect loose pucks and deposit them in the net. From 1983–84 to 1988–89, Kerr scored 48 or more goals in a season five times. "Kerr is an absolute load," said Pittsburgh Penguins defenseman Paul Coffey. "He drops that big behind of his in front of the net, and you need a bulldozer to root him out of there."

Bill Barber retired in **1985** as the club's all-time leading goal scorer (420 goals in 13 seasons).

The Flyers rode Kerr's scoring and the remarkable goaltending of Lindbergh to a 53–20–7 record in 1984–85. Philadelphia then powered its way to the Stanley Cup Finals, where it faced yet another dynasty—the defending champion Edmonton Oilers. Philadelphia won 4–1 in game one, but the Oilers regrouped to capture the Cup in five games. Sadly, the Flyers soon suffered a worse loss. Lindbergh, the 26-year-old goalie who had won the Vezina Trophy as the league's top netminder the year before, was killed in a car accident.

After the Lindbergh tragedy, the Flyers pulled together and returned to the Stanley Cup Finals in 1987, thanks largely to the

BILL BARBER

Physical, high-scoring winger Rick Tocchet was a Philadelphia standout of the **1980s**.

RICK TOCCHET

27
Brian's
VAUGHN
HEXTALL 27

play of another young goalie. Fiery Ron Hextall posted 37 wins in goal and carried the Flyers to the brink of a third championship. Facing Edmonton again in the finals, the Flyers fell behind three games to one before rallying to win the next two contests, forcing a game seven. The Oilers won the deciding game 3–1, but Hextall was so valiant in defeat that he won the Conn Smythe Trophy as the playoffs' Most Valuable Player.

No goalie guarded the Flyers' nets in more games than Vezina Trophy winner Ron Hextall (489 games).

{LINDROS AND THE "LEGION OF DOOM"} At the end of the 1989–90 season, the Flyers found themselves in an unfamiliar position—out of the playoffs. Injuries and age had taken their toll on the team, and with Tim Kerr finally slowing down, the Flyers were without a marquee scoring star.

The playoff drought continued through the 1993–94 season, but by then, the Flyers had a new star. On June 30, 1992,

RON HEXTALL

Philadelphia made one of the biggest trades in NHL history, sending goalie Ron Hextall, the rights to five top prospects, first-round draft picks in 1993 and 1994, and $15 million to the Quebec Nordiques

for the rights to rookie center Eric Lindros.

At 6-foot-4 and 240 pounds, Lindros represented the new wave of power players in hockey. Skilled and fast enough to weave his way through defenders, yet strong enough to blast right through them, Lindros was the biggest talent to enter the NHL in years.

The Flyers added more size with 6-foot-2 and 210-pound wing Mikael Renberg in 1993 and 6-foot-3 and 230-pound wing John LeClair in 1994. Together, the imposing trio became a scoring machine that left opponents beaten and bruised. By the end of the 1994–95 season, the Flyers were back in the playoffs, and the line of LeClair, Lindros, and Renberg had earned the ominous nickname, "The Legion of Doom." "It would be different if they were just big, or fast, or good around the net," said St. Louis Blues goaltender Grant Fuhr. "But all three of them can do it all."

Huge center Eric Lindros was awarded the Hart Trophy as MVP of the **1994–95** NHL season.

Philadelphia's return to prominence peaked during the 1996–97 season, when the Legion of Doom produced 94 goals and 131 assists. In the playoffs, the Flyers lost only three games in three

ERIC LINDROS

playoff series, reaching the Stanley Cup Finals for the seventh time in franchise history. But the Flyers' magic vanished in the finals, as the Detroit Red Wings swept the series.

From **1993** to **1999**, iron-man center Rod Brind'Amour played in 484 straight games.

{FLYING TOWARD THE FUTURE} The reign of the Legion of Doom ended when Renberg was traded in 1997. The Stanley Cup loss to the Red Wings had convinced Flyers management that the team needed better scoring balance instead of a reliance on one great offensive line.

The tinkering began to pay off in 1999–00, when Philadelphia roared to a 45–25–12 record. New Flyers such as big center Keith Primeau and speedy wing Simon Gagne, along with veterans Lindros, LeClair, and winger Mark Recchi, led the team to playoff wins over Buffalo and Pittsburgh.

Facing the New Jersey Devils in the Eastern Conference Finals, Philadelphia won three of the first four games before the Devils

R. BRIND'AMOUR

battled back to tie the series. In the first period of the deciding game seven, Lindros was knocked out with a concussion by a brutal check from Devils defenseman Scott Stevens. Without their star, the Flyers lost 2–1.

For Lindros, the injury was just the latest in a long series of concussions. Concerned about his health, Lindros sat out the 2000–01 season. While he was recovering, a long-simmering feud with team president Bobby Clarke boiled over. Before the 2001–02 season, Clarke traded Lindros to the New York Rangers for three players and a draft pick. "Eric didn't want to be in Philadelphia," said Clarke, "and I was more than happy to accommodate him."

Rising star Simon Gagne netted 27 goals in **2000–01** and played in his first All-Star Game.

To replace Lindros, the Flyers signed veteran center Jeremy Roenick. A six-time All-Star with the Chicago Blackhawks and Phoenix Coyotes, the high-scoring Roenick led the Flyers to another

SIMON GAGNE

JOHN LeCLAIR

In his first five full seasons in Philadelphia, John LeClair averaged 47 goals a year.

Durable winger Mark Recchi was equally skilled at shooting or passing the puck.

MARK RECCHI

division title in 2001–02. The season came to an abrupt end, however, when the Flyers were knocked out of the first round of the playoffs by the Ottawa Senators. After the loss, the team hired Ken Hitchcock as its new coach. Hitchcock had led the Dallas Stars to the Stanley Cup in 1999, and the Flyers and their fans were confident that he would take them to the top as well.

Flyers fans hoped to get a big offensive boost from young, 6-foot-5 center Michal Handzus.

The birthplace of the United States and one of the best hockey towns in the world, Philadelphia is a proud and historic city. For more than three decades, the city's hockey fans have seen star players, Stanley Cup championships, and a remarkable winning tradition that shows no signs of ending. With the support of the City of Brotherly Love, today's Flyers are hoping to soon soar to new heights.

MICHAL HANDZUS